Smidge

illustrated by
Jenny Arthur

meadowside
CHILDREN'S BOOKS

For Hannah.
B.S.

For Gid and the rest of my family,
but especially for Louie.
J.A.

First published in 2004
by Meadowside Children's Books
185 Fleet Street,
London EC4A 2HS

Text © Beth Shoshan 2004
Illustrations © Jenny Arthur 2004
The rights of Beth Shoshan and Jenny Arthur to be identified
as the author and illustrator of this work have been asserted by
them in accordance with the Copyright, Designs and Patents Act, 1988

A CIP catalogue record for this book is available
from the British Library
Printed in India

10 9 8 7 6 5 4 3 2 1

This
is Smidge.

Smidge likes to eat…

...a lot!

First, Smidge eats bags
of hot, red, sugar drops.

Then, Smidge eats fiery, yellow butterscotch.

Time for a rest.

So now Smidge eats ice-chilly,
blue-pepper, minty chews.

And then Smidge eats some mellow-yellow, jelly-bello beans.

Smidge is
feeling green…

This time Smidge eats bright red, dandy-candy drops and rooty-tooty, gooey-bluey fruit-bees.

Smidge feels mighty
bright and feisty purple.

But then (because they're there) **Smidge eats the hyper-stripey turbo toobs.**

And then (because Smidge never can say no)
**Smidge eats the hot and dotty,
super-spotty, speckled, spocked
and pickled pear drops.**

Followed by (they ARE winking at Smidge, after all) some cosmo-astral, decahedral, equilateral stellar stars. Which just don't seem the same without the roly-poly, extra round and eat-me-slowly, gorgeous, shmorgeous, quisquilious, hyper-fizzy, round and whizzy, chunky, mega-funky...

Smidge thinks *a pause might*

be a good idea.

hic!

Smidge doesn't feel hungry any more.